DATE DUE

D0891388

AUGURIES OF

INNOCENCE

AUGURIES OF

INNOCENCE

Patti Smith

An Imprint of HarperCollins Publishers

Glenview Public Library
1930 Glenview Road
Glenview, Illinois

HarperCollins books may be purchased for educational, business, or sales promotional use. For information please write: Special Markets Department, HarperCollins Publishers, 10 East 53rd Street, New York, NY 10022.

FIRST EDITION

Frontispiece and endpiece photographs copyright © 2005 by Patti Smith.

Library of Congress Cataloging-in-Publication Data
Smith, Patti.
    Auguries of Innocence : poems / Patti Smith.—1st ed.
    p. cm.
    ISBN-10: 0-06-083266-5
    ISBN-13: 978-0-06-083266-7
    I. Title.
PS3569.M53787L66 2005
811'.54—dc22

                                            2005048799

05 06 07 08 09 ❖/QWT 10 9 8 7 6 5 4 3 2

A skylark wounded in the wing,
A Cherubim does cease to sing.

WILLIAM BLAKE

CONTENTS

AUGURIES OF

INNOCENCE

THE LOVECRAFTER

I saw you who was myself
slightly stooped whistling mouth
with leather sack and breeches brown
striding the naked countryside

with summer bones long and dry
into the breadth of our glad day
mid afternoon the longer night
as you tread bareheaded bright

I saw you a wraith bemoan
stir the fires of the ancient ones
scarred with sticks pome and haw
as the nectar for their script

I saw you walk the length of fields
far as the finger of Providence
far as the mounds we call hills
ranges cut from the heart of slate

I saw you dip into your sack
scattering seeds where they may
as the woodsman hews his way
through oak ash and variant pines

for writing desks that shall reflect
a sheaf of lines that speak of trees
all sober hopes required within
all drunkenness as sacred swims

I saw the book upon the shelf
I saw you who was myself
I saw the empty sack at last
I saw the branch your shadow cast

WORTHY THE LAMB SLAIN FOR US

On the edge of a pasture in a confusion of stones,
obscured by the long grass and floramour,
the footprint of horror cloven and drawn.
She had a beautiful name: freedom.
Pretty little chop. Unmarketable, light
the bleating of new life.

He loved her mouth, tiny feet dressed in pleats.
Hearing her cry, he picked her up by the stem
of her throat in his thick arms slick with dew.
And he, a governed soul, broad shouldered
with eyes like Blake, lamented who bred thee, nursed
thee on mead and flowers, as he ripped her apart.

The barn was burning an indifferent hell,
engulfing little maids in their curly coats.
The field and fell lay empty as the heart.
He called to his god gasping for breath
we abandoned the farms we culled,
cut the cord, incinerated our little ones.

We did it for love we did it for man,
the hawthorn and the cuckoo,
the footpaths of Cumbria.
We did it for a beautiful name.
freedom, baa baa baa,
nothing you could put your finger on.

SLEEP OF THE DODO

The dodo sleeping, dreaming of himself,
lost in his daily doings. His wife mounted
in a menagerie of mogul extremes.
His children born and slain for sport,
with nary a nod save the wind,
echoing an old dance tune.

Funny squawks: coracoo, coracoo
swept by mist into the grotto,
the sugar plantation. Funny beaks
bobbing the swamp's dreaming pond.
Comic bodies washed up on the craggy
shore. Funny bones, then no more.

The sun hung, bled into the clouds.
God's bloodshot eyes, such sad surprise.
The dodo awoke, and seeing them,
slowly closed his own again.
Out of this world, into the indistinct
memory of a line that had forgotten itself.

THE LONG ROAD

Here we had best on tiptoe tread
While I for safety march ahead.
ROBERT LOUIS STEVENSON

We tramped in our black coats,
sweeping time, sweeping time,
sleeping in abandoned chimneys,
emerging to face the rain.
Wet, bedraggled, a bit gone,
trudging the grooves, chewing bulbs,
we were so hungry, tulips
blazed with ragged petals.

We adorned ourselves in pennywort,
slogged 'til spent the elected front,
the whisper of a trail we somehow knew,
rain that was not rain, tears not yet tears.

And the grail, oh the grail was just this close,
finished with foil, wrapped in sun.

Gladiolas were in bloom, bursting
from every crack. The whole world
anxious for holy mother to inspect
our chins with this familiar song—

Do you like butter?
Oh you like butter . . .

then set upon a hill yellow everywhere.

We mounted horses, rambled forests
mischievous fairies danced underfoot.
Branches snapped in our faces.

Our kingdom behind a chain link fence . . .

We grappled in the quarries, polished marbles,
knelt and shot for spoils in fervent circles.

We set up our furious camps,
our tents punctured with pegs,
nicked with pocket knives—
little foxes gauging the hard earth,
cursing the bottomland for making us soft.

We gathered rye, stuffed sacks, made pillows
for our men. We wrung the blood from soaking beds,
covered the martyrs' rolling heads, balanced
the buckets filled to the brim,
and we saw nothing and everything.

We rode on the back of the great bear, dipping our ladle
into the milky liquor spread like a white lake before us.

Our ships boasted obscenities scribbled
on parchment sails, floating illiterate rivers overturned
in bloody pools of rainwater muck.

We blew songs of praise into horns of sacred animals—
catcalls, confessions, teenage prayers
woven into tapestries of cloistered gardens.

No mother had we now, and rapping infinitesimal threads,
vows erupted with a new violence bearing no ill will
save to be born—our allegiance to motion
and the movement of the stars.

A blue light projected from the cap of a being
we could no longer name. We climbed the stairs
into a bluer heaven scarred with streamers,
bleeding the wind. We savored the spectacle.
Then it disappeared, but we were already gone.

We possessed a new radiance. Dew dropped
from our noses. We boasted shining skin,
shedding it without a sigh. Some raised their lanterns.
Some seemed to walk in a light of their own.

Fiery mounds that were not mounds, on the horizon . . .

Drawing closer we fell upon masses of greatcoats
abandoned by admiralty, deposed kings' purple,
medals of honor, regulation boots of dog tongue leather,
chits, animal hides, ermine and fleece worn by those
of high rank, princes and pilots, the magus and mystic.

Yet no rank had we fishing glad rags woven by the blind.
Ours was a country of sockets. They were empty.
And yet within one would find all a child hopes—
our own sweet story, our own sweet life,
cut with the cloth of ecstatic strife.

Once we knew where we were going, we leapt
in consecrated coats. We could have gone on forever
if not for this and that pulling at the starch of our sleeves.

We broke our mother's heart and became ourselves.
We proceeded to breathe and therefore to leave,
drunken, astonished, each of us a god.

Now you turn out the light.
Press your thumb to the wick.
If it sticks, you will burn.
If it goes poof, you will turn
into a beam that will extinguish
with the night into a dream
peppered with gimcracks.

We saw the eyes of Ravel, ringed in blue, and blinking
twice. We sang arias of our own, bummers chanting
dead blues of hallowed ground and mortal shoes,
of forgotten infantries and distances never dreamed—
yet only as far as a human hill, turned for wooden soldiers
stationed in the folds of blankets, only as far as a sibling's hand,
as far as sleep, a father's command—

   . . . the long road my children.

We broke from our moth husks alive in the night,
the sky smeared with stars we no longer see.
A child's creed stitched on handkerchiefs—

God does not abandon us
we are all he knows.
We must not abandon him,
he is ourselves
the ether of our deeds.

The whistling hobo calls, sweeping time, sweeping time.
We sleep. We scheme, pressing the vibrant string.
Happily self conscious, we begin again.

A PYTHAGOREAN TRAVELER

Awoke in a light not known before
the lodging's glass door mirroring
a likeness not hoped to glimpse again
clouds of my childhood, clouds of God
that supported the feet of Jesus Christ
ascending the brush of Raphael.

The young on their motorbikes do not lift
their heads nor cry: The clouds, the clouds.
They are always there—Mediterranean arias
mounting with swift and terrible calm.
Do they know me? Do they know I am here,
scribbling as they are decomposing?

The moon rises filled with moon blood
drawn from the Italian skies. Here Byron
unwound his turban and shook out his locks
as gulls dropped into the sea. The moon
knew her rival and hung like an ornament
from the ear of a bright deity curling his lips,
expelling great puffs, the clouds of San Remo.

I will sit here until dawn tripping the spine
of the stars, a Pythagorean traveler marveling
another numerical scheme, adding to his shoulder
a music not heard but attained.

Beauty alone is not immortal.
It is the response, a language of cyphers,
notes, and strokes riding off on a cloud charger—
the bruised humps of magnificent whales.
Clouds of my childhood, clouds of God
awash in rose, violet, and gold.

DESERT CHORUS

In the rich chorus of night, cosseted
beneath a web of diamonds, tiny
as mosquito eyes, a stranger mourns
the brevity of desert rain
a swaddled enemy's cries.

Soon the sun will ascend over Libya.
Can it matter? We have bombed
Benghazi. A dazed warhead struck
the compound of our foe lying alive,
his eyes white, black rimmed.
He could be heard crying in the desert
with arms now orphaned,
his infant swept into a burlap sack.
To what purpose?
The gold leaf of surrender?

The sun will ascend. Can it matter?
A poet sealed in skin disrobed, split.
Jean Genet, a thief in flight,
astray in the weave laid down
his arms spiraling in a length
of mosquito netting, dotted with eyes
of onyx, blinking above a one-star
Paris hotel indifferent to a bugger
a swaggering son of a bitch.
How shall his soul be redeemed
If not suffered by a little girl?

The dawn breaks the tempered heart
exposing a love for all things.
Hana Qaddafi, child of the flowers,
lead him across the violent threshold
where his marvelous pals await.
His prison a house of cards
collapsing in columns of roses—
a garland for your head.
Let your ashes anoint him.
He will magnify your name.
Opal hands gathering you
in a bridal train.

WRITTEN BY A LAKE

New Year's Day. Rain. Two candles light the room where they sleep. He writes. She confesses. This is where she weeps. She is the cause of the rain. She could not stop weeping and the sky obliged to follow.

(How is it mapped? What is the refrain? Why must the sky follow?) The heart drops in the center of an inexhaustible lake. How light the heart appears, yet how weighty a thing. A powerful stone carved in the shape of an organ with chambers pumping. How slick a shadow it leaks as its signature. Sticky, oxblood, the color of new shoes. High topped, gold laced and worn with expectations poised to ride out life on horseback. Racing from hill to hill with humor, horror, bits of Spanish stitched on sleeves.

The work wrung with this cry. Look you radiant wash yard. The sheets billow. Their wet folds tell a tale. Once there was a girl who walked straight, yet she was truly lame. She walked upright in new boots, yet I tell you her feet were bare. She lives forever, yet she lies buried in a vault of fertile air.

New Year's Day. The wicks twist. The insistent mirror winks. An eye with time as her lashes. And if he—slipping at last, face pressed against the glass, releasing beads of spittle from parting lips—should suddenly speak, what would he say? And if she, shaken from her torpor, should rise to write, what would she write? Their table is laid with the promise of the lake. Water sighs for want of blood. It is nothing. These remains, malleable ash, are nothing. Signs for want of substance. A sack of sticks spilling order upon the surface. Words traced on a slab hewn from another forested mind.

a postscript prefiguring—

Your fingers press the door triggering a spring exposing the hard corner where you have walked. You shall not stumble. Offer a fist encasing rivets extracted from the wet pout of this time or that. Prick the hour's hand with nothing but eyes. Think nothing of it. For what remains to flush is nothing but salt jamming the mechanism of formal delights, former misery. Nothing but salt to bundle and fling over a shoulder. Nothing but clumps of salt to toss, years later, like dice across a board of glass where you'll sit on a ledge circling a glowing body, unfastening the dressings of a burden gone. The cremation of all my sorrow—may you spread the singed grains with your fingers, and without thought brush them aside.

Thus free to drown in sorrow of your own, may you sit in the shadows of our lost life, immersed in stillness, flanked by translucent hills, one a mountain coated immaculate and ringed at the throat with beads of cloud.

These words were written by a lake.

String them around a wrist. Do not grip a sword or draw what might be drawn, for wisdom is a dying bird, engraved on a palm. Next to nothing. And these words were written by a lake, before being as being was scripted and dealt. A pack of lives, each with a winning face, each with this blushing command:

Prick this. This moment the hand is free.

THE ORACLE

He was a stone boy divined by his sister.
She slept standing while he by the rim
played with a ball the color of water,
gazing all reason therein.

He was summoned to the sibylline barren,
carried by sweetness his mouth drew the spring.
They rejoined through the ball of water,
patterns foreshadowing.

Darts of fortune scattered unnoticed,
flew like the raven in a twisting scrawl.
His transitive senses he left to his sister.
Her tears were the color of stone boy's ball.

THE SETTING AND THE STONE

The setting is a barren place
colorless, with dry purple shrubs,
small rocks sheaved in light
and dust, dust everywhere.
The stone is betrayal,
rich, energetic,
the color of an elf's slipper.

He skips over the landscape,
his tiny tracks alive
with the lustrous fibers
of his soles:

The red beat of betrayal.

Three halves and the moon
is suddenly undone.
The mountain knows this,
as do all the idols
laughing at our futile efforts
to be whole, to be holy
without them.

The ring around our neck
has a weight, a weight.

Look, the prophet waltzed
this arid place and baptized
it with his sweat.
He was mad, by God.
Naked, he tread vipers
and felt nothing.

Yet he was drawn
from the smooth
crown of the locust
into Herod's nest,
the palace of lust,
a teen-age dance.
She encircled him.
and he lost his head.

THE MAST IS DOWN

We lay in the cursed grass devoid of magic,
tracing our disintegration in the kinetic sky.
I touched your arm and the flesh fell away,
and my hands were no longer empty.
Our mount is made of blood earth,
when wet a clay thing writhing.
If you breathe in its mouth it will fly
above the Moorish towers into the blue.
The *Pinta* is a ship the lone navigate,
channeling the mind once beguiled.
I touched your hip, the bone fell away
and the sea was no longer empty.
We love yet reclaim our dark sails,
gorging the belly of a red dog.

THE BLUE DOLL

This morning I dreamed you returned and left a blue doll face down on my mother's quilt. I reached to turn it over, as a black liquid seeped from a crack in the wall and bled into a pool, rising beneath our bed. The doll had blue hair and a blue face. I gripped it by the ankles and shook it like a medicine rattle. I shook it with such force, the head spun and I felt remorse.

I rose and fastened my hair. My robe trailed the rim of the black water. My nose began to bleed, slowly at first, then tear sized drops that slid down my throat, staining my collar and bodice. My dress was the dress on the blue doll. I walked on the water through the walls into the forest to a rocky hillock. I cut a path and ascended barefoot.

I lay face down on the crest, humming the music of a fluted sun. I was no longer angry. I was no longer than the span of a note sounded by a thrush in the wood.

EVE OF ALL SAINTS

The writer who did not write moved by feel alone, was eaten by his words, by drink, his own hand casting a line, drawing empty river. He felt a glow, not his, wrapping around him in the tavern—a silent salute from the strangers he loved and who loved him.

The writer who did not write suffered to return, dragging his foot. The willows swayed a greeting, ever so slightly. The shouts of little beggars, with their sacks and jack o' lanterns, spilled through the dusk as they flew past him, trampling the marigolds growing wild on his dead end street.

She held the screen door open, as he approached the laughter of their children, the spoils of their pillowcases, fruits and candy soul cakes spread across the floor. He stepped over their masks—handkerchiefs with holes for eyes—and hobo shoes. The potatoes had yet to be peeled. His shirts were rinsing in the sink. He felt within his cheek and extracted a tooth, an ivory charm, for his love to wrap in silver paper. In her hand, beating like a small drum, he placed it.

The writer who did not write mounted the stairs. His children watched him faltering, his feet going on him. She followed and lay down beside him. He rested his head on her shoulder. A macabre magic filled the air. Little beggars raced from house to house, calling "trick or treat," ringing bells, lacing the bushes with long veils of tissue. He dreamed of a fishing tournament, a musky strung up on the back of a truck. It was a lucky day for the old fisherman and he felt strung up as well and still aglow. It came in waves in his sleep—labor without pain. No life. No life anywhere and the blood had a metallic smell like a freshly painted *retablo* framed in flowers, carved in sugar.

She clipped a lock of his brown hair and wrapped it in the silver paper, with his tooth and a gold ring. She made a reliquary of him. His half-empty can she drained into the mouth of the river. She flattened the tin and painted a fish hanging in the green sky. She sat in the grass where they sat in the night. The willows swayed a greeting, ever so slightly, as she prayed, not to God, but to him. The stars scattered like a rosary suddenly unstrung. Medals embossed with saints rained upon the grass. The little beggars filled their sacks with them and handed one to her—St. Federico, the writer who does not write, the patron of forsaken fields.

> *My dove,* your name is water in my hand.
> I will offer it with salt and bread and the charm extracted
> without resistance from your silent mouth.
> I will canonize your name for mysteries unsolved,
> words unborn,
> because you suffered, my *calavera,* my sad, sad saint,
> my writer who did not write.
> Because your beautiful sorrow sprouted like a stalk,
> blossoming calligraphy.

SHE LAY IN THE STREAM DREAMING OF AUGUST SANDER

You, I write beloved black ace Ophelia
extravagantly pierced dread pale moon.
Negatives inflame your immutable eye,
hands face feather soaked in love.

Cast your pearls pen the pink fat night.
Comb ashes from the garden asylum,
the white cliff of ambition shedding.
Shoot baby shoot, powers can alter.

Her human cathedral hung with tassels
of hair threaded with golden string.
And she sang as she slid dangerously alive
through long arms of trailing algae.

I have collected children. I have felt
the museum fled that mountain—viewed
with suspicion memories snowing.

the white cliff of ambition

in those soft trine

She unfastened the strings and fruit erupted.
The flayed mule became one with her,
they lay uncorrupted in the deep grass
pecked palm to palm by ebullient fowl.

You are my summer knight she whispered.

The spokes of the wheel bear witness.
A barren heart is a heart that does not choose.
Beloved, come down fluid like naked convinced
a heart has stopped floating orchid child.

Horns of angel turned in virulent dust,
being to feel found shelter in fire.
The first roar dry and blood brown
crisscrossing the kingdom of a wrist.

FOURTEEN

There will always be devotion,
smoke coiling the open wound,
snaking the deep loam, molding
a clay head twittering the end.
There will always be romance,
the tit and the mouse,
and the defecating louse.

A curtain drops cabbage-edged,
anklets slouching schoolgirl shoes.
She tiptoes the stage, curtsies
her closing piece and purses
a mirror anticipating a kiss.
Invective pours an unruly mouth.
She is as hard as you, hard
as your dreams rolled between
fingers, bled out of the blue.

Fourteen, each year a station crossed.
Her head droops, a capricious rose
crushed by gravity. How so and why
sours the tiny bud. She was fouled
in the leaves and the negative space
between them burnt into tears. She was
fouled in the leaves and the earth
shuddered, as the clay heads spoke.

What will we learn from all these words?

There will always be smoke, a satchel
of crumbling verbs, lusted by gods,
devoured by birds as they hit the sky—
their bellies full of India ink,
tales of assassins, the death of a pink,
extracting from its scalloped heart
pollen that could bruise a child's cheek.

Clambering, grasping a small handful
of grass, poets and liars moan in the glass—
the glare masking the green of her eyes,
that moisture absorbed, the salt of the sky.
They sing of her lovely life,
what a number she is, a form of prime
strung like stars circling the throat
of a petulant muse whose crinolines
test cultures' wriggling death.

BIRDS OF IRAQ

March twentieth
awake spring.
The birds are silent.
It is happening again.
I rise yet cannot rise.
I take to my bed
wind the sheet
about my head.
It is coming on
a nerve storm
triggering
the current
source of suffering
stones pelting
the human spring.
And I am myself.
And I am another.
And now my mother
stretched retching
in a bucket
fan spinning overhead
her children in a row
observing by the door
with scientific wonder
they've seen it before.
No dinner no story.

Hammering the wall
wet cloths and balm
hennaed strands
soaked in sweat
loosening her sun dress
barely casing toppled flesh
howling Jesus
Mary and Joseph
my head my head.
I the eldest
administering
in dutiful silence
condemned
as I am now
administering myself
grasping the towel
the storm in the air
is also my brow.

Yesterday
the nineteenth
her birthday
St. Joseph's day.
She will not
return as swallows
to perch on a rock

in Capistrano
with the casual
symmetry
of a setup
a shooting gallery
bird heads
plopping
basket of ironing
that I will have to do.
Throbbing images
melodies looping
mother wailing
our childish games.
Can't I have some peace?
Can't I have some peace?
Can't I have some ice?

What are they doing
wild little mice
bombing
the first day
of spring?
Baghdad
the city of peace
the caliph and the thief.
I remember nights

swept by the sea.
I read the Waves
but never ventured in
the polio epidemic.
Indians don't swim.
They worship the tides
and they are coming in.

Virginia praying for night
refusing to be black
for the moon is full
spilling the skylight
dripping voices
or are they birds?
Why did they cease chirping?
When will I cease retching?
And how did my head
learn to swim?

The equinox passed.
She marched
to the river.
A letter for L.
A letter for V.
Stone by stone
the ring ouzel

and starry rooks
the weeds floating
the pitted mirror
a glimpse of gone
a quiet hand
twisting a sheet
between her teeth
pleading amnesty
whispering
nervous hummingbirds
dreaming of asylum
Saint-Rémy
impossible peace
hammering inventory
ruthless embroidery
painted trays
ambulance spattered
in Julian's blood.
Madder palette knife.
Discard possessions.
Cut hair cut hair.
Rose growing annuals
thorny hair
would not stop
piercing her scalp
thick-walled gardens

Vanessa in heaven
Thackeray's great
glass-fronted cabinet.
It was a dream.
It was her head
hammered head.
And she wonders
how could I think
such a violent thing?
How could I think
such a violent thing?
And Buddha
was unaware of Isaiah.
And Isaiah unaware
of Heraclitus.
Yet all existed
in the same moment.
And who exists as we exist?
Fingers inch by inch
spread the country of her bed
through the window
shattered cabinet glass
shams wet with tears
spittle and sweat
desperate eyes
clasping vines

counting beans
the murmur of leaves
a history of the world
written on the humps
of broken beasts.
The birds are silent
before they cease
before the bough breaks.
Iraq spring awake.
Bombs fall like fruit.
The peach trees
lining the boulevard
behind the mosque
in flames
the hoopoe
the turtle dove
showering
remains
spattering sheets
children toting guns
women soldiering.
And I am not them
wrapped in muslin
bric a brac flying
no connection
no culminating

piece of action
no end no end.

Over the Tigris
the Euphrates
helicopters
drop leaflets
for people to eat.
They paper the moon
the hammered mind.
What century is this?
Truly the last
as camels race
freed from embroidered
vests and leather saddles
sacks of spice
and water gourds.
They run and the sun
explodes.
The lamb of god bleats.
Goats separate from the sheep
their beards are woven
into scarves
adorning priests and freaks.
Camels in the dust
astonished by their wounds

their racing minds
Ata Allah—bedouin name
their small ears lined with fur
filter dust and sand
double row of curly lashes
shields their large soft eyes
from the desert sand
hair they shed in spring
highly sought
for artists' brushes
Vanessa's
Duncan's.

The band tightened
around my head
slid, encircled my wrist.
I couldn't write
couldn't grasp
a single thing
not word
nor world
just time
beading
a long
fragile
string.

When you snap
a neck
something stops
turning in
a jewel box
beneath a hammered lid.
We met in the spring house
enacted our play
slept in a tent of sheets
and dreamed of the desert.
We heard the call to prayer
and the sky was magic.
Men were leading camels.
We knelt in the thorny scrub
and when I awoke
there were scratches
on my knees.
And never again
will vision be so acute
that dreams could
produce blood
a thorny path
littered with wings.
If we tape them
to our shoulders
surely we could fly.

We would be free
like the hoopoe
like the curlew
singing in spring.
Are you coming
my sister?
Are you coming?
Mother's better.
We are flying
on our own
flapping
up and down
up and down
discarding
sweaters
baring
arms.
Oh
to be
so small.

TO HIS DAUGHTER

What is the heart but a small hand,
of agonies? What is the immobile
stag, but a blessing disguised
within the pages of a book?

Little one, set down your hymnal,
rest it upon your knee. Tears
may stain the fragile leaf,
let them fall, let them fall.

Your father has rushed forth
in a column of mist. Now you seek
him in columns of words, water
and stone. He is here little heart.

The stag fell under the stroke
and into a blackness
so bright as to fold
light. Here. Pressed between

hymn and hymn a perfect thorn,
the spear of your father's love.
The hart faltered and fell.
The red-skinned hart.

He is the gust that lifts a bit of sail
to press your cheek, wipe the tears.
A bit of sail without moral, turning
like an apron upon a cloud.

THE PRIDE MOVES SLOWLY

I heard you crying in your sleep
and stood above your contour there.
I saw the moon behind your ear,
wrists as mine, my mother's hair.

I saw you with your father's arms
and so possess his blades,
protruding like small wings
I thought I'd never see again.

The lamp of his boyhood glows,
the pride moves slowly
as in a dream. Circling
the shade's lucent plain.

Bequeathed with certain calm,
the outline of their forms
diffuse as memories stream,
sown in sadness, sleep.

THE LEAVES ARE LATE FALLING

The leaves are late falling, the plane trees
gowned as to partner air.

Star to star, they hold fast in the cold
light filtering music.

Two hands ago these fingers were yours,
folding a guitar placed by our son

closing his eyes, a metronome pacing
the percussion of an errant wind

as the lid fastened, marking time,
year's mind and mind's end.

In a circle, on a rise, currents waltz
the restive plane,

their gowns loosening, they fall
one by one shimmering,

signing as their word
that somewhere you are good.

WILDERNESS

Do animals make a human cry
when their loved one staggers
fowled dragged down
the blue veined river

Does the female wail
miming the wolf of suffering
do lilies trumpet the pup
plucked for skin and skein

Do animals cry like humans
as I having lost you
yowled flagged
curled in a ball

This is how
we beat the icy field
shoeless and empty handed
hardly human at all

Negotiating a wilderness
we have yet to know
this is where time stops
and we have none to go

THE GEOMETRY BLINKED RUIN
UNIMAGINABLE

She clawed through the rubble of her world
head covered a scrupulous maid searching for gems
a necklace mislaid by her mistress on the marble floor
of a ballroom set against the battered sky

She crawled with her babe limp as a doll in floral crayon
fleeing hell straight into the light of her ancestors

She crawled through arches suspended
wrapped her babe in the shawl she had worn
to market no more than a scar on the face of a hill
hair ribbons fluttering girders blood silk
oozing the wounded sky shot with holes
foxes scuttling crackling wires
patches of honey colored coats shivering
down mixed with bits of calico and flesh

She crawled a chessboard a cage of gold
scaffolding she crawled with her face oblique
placed her babe before the altar of the Art of War

She picked through the remnants of the Basque
countryside a cockeyed dress-maker
piecing a pattern gone awry

Through the rubble she crawled
with one shoe the other foot gone
a trail sticky and warm

She crept into the belly of a fallen horse
drawing its life into her mouth
covering her doll with kisses
she knelt entreating her god
an immense crucifix swathed
in telegraph wire that spun
like a bottle in the center of a circle

She made a sign over her breast
and stuffed her mouth with biscuits

Body of Christ . . . Body of Christ

Horses wept jewels the size of fists
swept by scholars with a mind
to twist and level facets
of each plane to be raffled
when the bombing ceased

Before the Art of War she laid her babe

To be raffled with the heart of the artist
bulldozed crucified then razed again

to house an outstretched arm
hoof and thigh reins that ran scarlet
streaming the horse's knotted mane

dripping blood from the wounds of Christ
dripping blood from the wounds of Spain

Black and white blood dripping

The ghost of Sophia pranced in her rag dress
through walls of glass—the unspeakable

The hairs on his forearms bristled the sense
of her pressing in like a dosed handkerchief

He picked up a stick and covered fresh sheets

Dripping the hardened horn
Dripping the indignant ring

Slaughter flower dead child hoof capacious eye
lighting the halls of the Spanish pavilion

He bore down on the stick to canvas spent
and on the seventh day he wept

FENOMENICO

The music of the spheres knew not of what it sang.
The flame of love mounts quicker than the flame of sacrifice.
This flame burns slow and the body consumed holds its form
a small slumping figure stripped and shorn
mouthing the words: "Jesus, Jesus."

She reached, not with her bound hands, but with her eyes.
The sacrifice made on the cross harmonized with her own.
Her banner, intact, hung from the arches of the sky.

I sat in a square humming a song of the shepherd girl
who rose above her station to liberate her king.
Yet he abandoned her to secular authority
and she languished in chains
a daughter of deep neglect.

Her *harnois blanc* lay upon the altar
Her *difformitate habitus* shredded immaculate
Her broken sword, an *ex-voto*, caught in the bramble
the sweetbriar enmeshed in sad soldier thread.

I reached to touch but was moved by the rustling gowns
of the conclave; the lapping of the *Apostolic See.*
A moat encircled the *Duomo* and I noticed a small boat
laden with bread and fishes.

I reached for the oar but was suddenly drawn by the
geometric design paving the wide quadrangle of the *piazza*.
The mosaic sang beneath my feet as I entered an ancient
garden winding the heart of the perennial cycle.

⌐⌐

A long-stemmed *boccolo* with magnificent thorns appeared
before me. I knelt to claim it when I saw you standing by
the column of the winged lion in your overcoat, smiling.
A golden ball balanced above the tumulus
like a small planet eaten away by a spiral mist.

The music of the spheres knew not of what it sang yet
filled the heavens with a bold and jubilant silence.
I felt the lantern of your arm
the pageantry of your breath
the source of an exquisite wound.

THREE WINDOWS

In the garden of the fugitive
he knelt singing
I am with thee

In his white cassock he cried
I pray for that brother
who shot me

A black crucifix appeared
as he lay dying
forgive me

I am one

Crepe streamed from three windows
a flag dropped bound in mourning
these words entered the heart

You have come
the door is open
you will not find me
you will find my love

OUR JARGON MUFFLES THE DRUM

Children marching scraps of humanity beating their drum of blood rushing streets buried alive on the moral high ground burned in their beds in the name of crusades not sanctioned by law any savior at all small limbs severed in the name of gods fleeing holocaust streets of the wrong dawn blighted angels swarming burrows wading sewage sleep of the ragged caged glue sniffing packs of the dogged pinned and glazed and bound by fashion rubber shoes stitched by child hands and where shall they dream dancing splintered streets naked feet with none to remove slivers of fiery ice to warn hearts underfoot to wash the tears of children streaming by twos and tens and tens of thousands with small hands open to fallout follies frozen embryo stem cells blown promises lowered into plundered shafts and children are swarming mounting refrigerators no more cookie jar just rounds of ammo to pump into their pals by the grace of our stupidity they say we have your guns your lack of recognition that we are children and we mimic like parrots and we are going to play you taking down all in our wake in a pink buzz on the way of swollen bellies enslaved ignored skewered abhorred embedded in the new century that has abandoned their hands prayer common mind signs worth deciphering code worth dying words worth living force fed fast food educated by tube entertained with sex scandal serial killer white supremacists and

gaudy rappers spoiled like carcasses of studded beef swinging
in the sun shot by princess deprived paparazzi grieving images
icons blown by fame by their own silver hand jobs presidential
blow job mourning the death of stars while babes are left in
swaddling heaps babes to languish in streets of blurring mists
not parted nor blessed and the children coming with their hands
outstretched and we fill them with stinging amendments mate-
rial rites non patriot acts to play entrap avenge revenge yet there
is a higher flower waiting to be plucked a recompense worthy
of their pure palm and it contains nothing but itself to raise the
head of the son to bathe in lucid milk drink the radiance within
the stream and the children are racing streets with no name
besieged streets of the veil of the blue mosque streets of the
jubilant damned street of the nailed the pawned profiteer street
of the prophet hanged man rapist priest amorphous children
glowing from dark to dark to dark and the way of the bread
and the empty hand of innocence transfusing street of the
sorrows and children of the wood hounded shredding all veils
unwinding all sheets of the dead world droning overturning
tables laden with silver sacrificial birds beating goatskin drums
advancing with hands outstretched and we keep filling them
with mercury nitrate asbestos baby bombs blasting blue scav-
engers picking through the ashes of city of the dead exploited

raging children of the mills children of the junkyard malls
trafficked children high risk asylum children orphaned abused
shining children damned and gifted blind scorned and beautiful
toughs funneling traumatized hungry for lullabies sucked
through the shafts sleepy illiterate fuzzy little rats haunted paint
snuffers stoned out of their shaved heads forgotten foraging
sex slaves sleeping urine and excrement gutter saints mystical
children foul mouth glassy eyed hallucinating hallowed nameless
soldier blitzing the pure street of the numb with outstretched
hands and children are raging like packs of dogs and who shall
feed them shall serve up centuries of love lost as they squat in
our shit unable to comprehend their own beneath constellations
of fear as we wield vanities gesturing extinction and the children
are mouthing natures small agonies and fish are writhing in the
desert and the sea no longer shining sea and mountains shall
be razed erupting small fingers tracing the end of things and
children are marching beating their drums of blood joined by
ghosts offering sweet cornflowers to fold and stuff the cheek of
the future tiny fists signaling take heed thee guardian for none
shall be first and none shall be last and who shall greet the sun if
the air be pink with folly and who shall remain save the children
of the game and they shall be as bread upon the earth and they
shall build monuments to the saints of their day and they shall

shed all veils unwind all flags and hail their mother who found
them naked abandoned in coffin shaped baskets and lifted them
bathed and clothed them in the finery of her love and they shall
remember her in cloth of blue dawn anchored in faith bathed in
hope with charity unfurled as they rebuild our world.

DEATH OF A TRAMP

The hills were green and so were we
but not in the way men talk about
we had not known death
nor walked with stain
for all was bright about the hand

We had not known death
yet the sparrows ring
set like a wreath upon the marsh
marked for all that shivered cross
in cast-off clothes himself cast-off

In sun and wind his tramping drum
the high grass knew his shuffling
kindness wrapped his being mild
his countenance moved the brethren

The stench and sense of aimless wrath
now we know death not so the man
a wildflower stowed in ragged breast
the hills are grieved their innocence

MUMMER LOVE

Come in lovely Mummers don't bother the snow
We can wipe up the water sure after you go
Sit if you can or on some Mummer's knee
Let's see if we know who ya be
TRADITIONAL

A face pressed to mine. A black hole planting a kiss, an uproari-
ous cry. It was not cruelty, not even insult, but a quirky form of
universal love. An impulse of great narcotic joy. One of the lower
orders, a lone mummer from Conception Bay, engaging in horse-
play far from home. He pressed his face to mine, then staggered
away, howling, while I, small and reproachful, tried to wipe away
the smear of a vague initiation into the festival of life.

I fled the masquerade through ranks of grotesque string bands
shaking down Market Street. Through the heart of Philadelphia
I ran, toward City Hall, topped with the imposing figure of
William Penn breathing upon my startled being.

Brothers in blackface splendidly clad chasing small boys and
whipping their legs. Gaudy tattlers parading the streets and per-
forming rude dances. Strays dragging plumes in the slush
splashing as little ice crystals formed in my socks.

I did not join the other children throwing pennies on Ben
Franklin's grave, crying *good luck*, *good luck*. But something
struck me as I scraped the clover from my shoes. Why should

there be clover? I was driven to the snow. Why should there be clover—each one four leaved, boasting the luck of his caste?

I was left to wonder of this raucous swarm why I, in my plaid coat and little watch cap, was chosen by the King of Fools for a bristly greasepaint kiss. It set me apart, in heart, year to New Year. Assailed by winter fever, no longer dead, I vainly attempted to peel the mug of mummer love.

My coat reeked, my face sooty with indignant tears. It didn't really matter then. It doesn't really matter now. I can make it matter or not. I can be beatific or dead. I can be bountiful or a shriveled branch. I long to see, to hear that which I create. The moods storm the impossible sink flushing water the wrong way corkscrew style. I long to hear that which I made and not outlive it. Not outlive it.

oh stolen book my salvation no crime sweet no scent mesmeric
no snow so light than the simple knowledge of you rimbaud
sailor face words hidden in my blouse so close to my breast
—piss factory draft

The years saw me grow long-limbed awkward inexplicably maverick. I sought my kind and found none. How you rescued me. Your peasant hands reaching through time wrapping my young heart. Your poems, found in a stall by the greyhound station I dogged dreaming of escape, were my ticket out of my cloistered existence. Words I could not comprehend and yet, deciphered by blood, illuminated adolescence. Armed with you I fled the rural suffocation of southern New Jersey past the streets of our forefathers to New York City of poet rats and public transit. I wrote with the image of you above my worktable, vowing to one day trace your steps dressed in the watch cap and coat of my present self.

This morning, pulling into your town, I walked the streets that you despised, the streets I love for your having despised them. I sleep steps away from your child sleep and awake to hear you call. I sense you loitering by the river, willing me to rise.

I will go to the train station in Roche, touch the remains of the wall of the farmhouse where you wept *A Season in Hell* while your sisters harvested the fields.

I will walk the road you raced as a sturdy-limbed boy. The road you were carried on with one leg, facedown on a litter, flanked by misery who loved no company—the road to Marseilles, to a ship returning to Abyssinia, to descend into the abyss, the black hole of universal love.

I will be there at the station in Roche. I will piss in the urinal you pissed in. A young man cursing existence. And then a dying man. I will squat and rise. I will stand. I will give you my limbs, no longer young, but sturdy all the same.

Mummers ask for nothing in return. They give a sign to sign. Then they're gone. I project from the urinal to Marseilles that you gave glory and they just tossed it away into the river—a discarded wreath where rats sit, using it for a nest. A. Rimbaud, the rats' poet laureate.

⌁

A rat is all I have been, scurrying through the streets of the city of brotherly love. I am here my brother. I am here where you were and I feel as if I could find you waiting, if I only drew myself from this torpor and moved into the empty streets. I know your loneliness, which I desired to fill with my own. But I am no longer lonely. I am this close to a shade. Yet I still feel. I long to peel the last of my face struck in mummer love and left the impression of a festival. To the new. To the new year. And it's not clear at all why it embedded itself in me. That phantom clown chose me, unformed. He left me branded forever it seems, until perhaps, this moment while I peel the last face. The last phase of my existence. As you read. As I have written. As I have gone.

⌁

Seedless winter. Yet it springs with life. There should be fireworks. It's Independence Day. The sky, which I cannot see, is alive with colored wheels and I know saints have been stretched on such glowing racks. Girls as sweet as stems and gloomy priests. Everything compressed into a leaf pressed in a book. The book of summer, when I wrote about winter. The book of life that told of the dead. Everyone wears a corpse about their wrist. Just a bit of twine, but a corpse all the same. A dead thing proclaiming I have you and you. I will snip all these things and hurl all rings in the urinal you knelt in. Your tears made it over-flow. All the sewage covered the station and made you shudder. This was as close to a laugh as you could get. The image of a shit-covered wagon. You stood clad in white, trembling.

Once I awoke and heard your voice. I caught bits of nature in truth, our whole natural world. I heard the dead. They were calling to me. I felt my powers. Yet I did not go out into the night. I did not go out into the world. I did not use my powers but I wrote what I wrote. My heart cries but my eyes are dry as a salt bed.

The cursed mist shall lift and all the infants' breath. I will butter my hair. I will unfasten the last. I will tremble like you when I glimpse the visible ink peeling at the edge of my cheek. I have danced on the edge of ignorance. I have wept impossible dreams. I have melted nothing. I have stood in the warped curve of a light that should have taken me away yet left me with the human kind I have never been.

Everything here is a small offense and not of value as art or confession. It is not a whim. It is an attempt to peel another putrid skin. The greasepaint of mummer love. The honor and the stain. So when it happens, I can say I did it. I'll be okay. Just a kid. A severely gimped little goat, yet sturdy limbed, who can hold you up. The goats once ran wild over the cobblestone streets of the city of brotherly love. And I am as they on your road my brother.

Who can color a corpse around the wrist and call it blessed? All because of mummer love. One deep and scratchy greasepaint kiss on the day of the new and spotless. This is what I know. I am here for a purpose. The purpose changes. Gifts that are not mine. Children who are not mine. An angel who is not mine. And this—to meet you at the urinal and draw you upright in my arms. I am still sturdy. This memory may enter me and I will realign the clay of my being. Will be you. Muscle shall be ours. All limbs intact. All brutal mirrors cracked. I am here and that is something. I am here my friend, and have always been. As much as for any living thing.

THE WRITER'S SONG

I did not wish to work
I did not wish to earn
but to curl with my jar
in the sweet sorghum
I laid my mat among the reeds
I could hear the freemen call
oh my life
what does it matter
will the reed cease bending
will the leper turn
I had a horn I did not blow
I had a sake and another
I could hear the freemen
drunk with sky
what matter my cry
will the moon swell
will the flame shy
bonsai bonsai
it is better to write
then die
in the blue crater
set with straw
I could hear
the freemen call
the way is hard
the gate is narrow
what matter I say

with the new mown hay
my pillow
I had a sake and another
I did not care to own nor rove
I wrote my name upon the water
nothing but nothing above
bonsai bonsai
it is better to write
then die
a thousand souvenirs
a thousand prayers
set away in earthenware
we draw the jars
from the shelves
drink our parting
from ourselves
so be we king
or be we bum
the reed still whistles
the heart still hums

This book was set in Fournier, a typeface made by Monotype in 1924. The design is based on types cut by Pierre Simon Fournier, circa 1742, some of the most influential designs of the eighteenth century. Fournier's types were among the earliest of the "transitional" style of typeface and are seen as a link to the more severe "modern" style made popular by Bodoni later in the century. They had more vertical emphasis than the old-style types, greater contrast between thick and thin strokes, and more subtle serifs. Fournier has a light, clean look on the page and is legible and elegant for text.

Designed and composed by Jessica Shatan Heslin

Printed and bound by Quebecor World